The Death of *Evening Star*

The Death of *Evening Star*

The Diary of a Young New England Whaler

written and illustrated by
LEONARD EVERETT FISHER

Doubleday and Company
New York

ISBN: 0-385-07649-5 TRADE
0-385-08631-8 PREBOUND
Library of Congress Catalog Card Number 75-164719

All that we call lives and souls,
lie dreaming, dreaming, still;
tossing like slumberers in their
beds; the ever-rolling waves but
made so by their restlessness.
                    Herman Melville (1851)

The Death of *Evening Star*

PART I
A STRANGE TALE BRIEFLY TOLD

I never knew Captain Jeremiah Poole, master of the bark *Pandora,* a whaleship out of New Bedford, Massachusetts. That is, I never knew him when he was alive—at least I do not think so.

The log of the *Pandora* records that Captain Jeremiah Poole, age seventy-three, died aboard his ship on September 6, 1901. That was the day President William McKinley was shot in Buffalo—and that was long before I was born. Captain Poole was bringing the *Pandora* home to New Bedford with a rich cargo of whale oil and bone after having been at sea several years when he was fatally stricken. He was buried at sea fifty nautical miles due east of Sandy Hook, New Jersey.

Nevertheless, Captain Jeremiah Poole invaded my conscious-ness and, indeed, my very life in a strange and eerie way. It all began back in the late 1930s. It was then that I met Jeremiah Poole—or rather his only son, Amos—or was it Amos?

Amos Poole, by his own admission, was a retired naval officer. He was well past eighty when I first set eyes on him. Like his father before him, Amos Poole was a seafaring man and lived in New Bedford. For some three or four years, usually during the summer months, he would travel to New York City to visit with *his* only son, Charlie, keeper of the Norton's Point Lighthouse.

The lighthouse was then—and still is—a landlocked gleaming white cylinder supported by a mammoth tripod capped by a glass-walled pagoda housing a great lamp. It rises above the low landscape on a fenced-off half acre of the most southwesterly edge of Brooklyn—a point of land in New York City that separates Gravesend Bay from the Atlantic Ocean. The entire community—a crowded private enclave nestled on a grassy tract of sand and soil behind and to both sides of the lighthouse—is called Sea Gate.

I lived with my parents and brother nearby. Frequently, I would wander over to the soaring steel column hoping to be invited up the winding staircase to enjoy the sweeping view and to inspect the giant bulb. But nothing ever came of it.

I knew Charlie Poole as well as anyone in the neighborhood and that is not saying very much. Charlie never invited anyone inside the lighthouse grounds. He kept to himself, tended the light, a few chickens he had and otherwise came and went in mysterious silence. Usually, he could be seen prowling around the circular gallery at the top of the lighthouse. Occasionally, he would halt his constant pacing and train a pair of powerful binoculars on the not too distant reaches of Sandy Hook and the rolling ocean to the east—the site of his grandfather's watery grave. His view was clear and unobstructed in good weather.

Charlie, his chickens, his clapboard home and the lighthouse were all protected from the curious public by a solid wood fence and a sign which said:

U. S. GOVERNMENT PROPERTY
KEEP OUT
TRESPASSERS SUBJECT TO
ARREST FINE AND IMPRISONMENT

That was enough for me. I kept out. But I was never very far away.

One warm summer morning I strolled over there, hopeful as ever. Hardly had I settled my elbows on the fence when I was startled by the sudden appearance of a bony hulk of a man directly in front of me and not more than six inches from my nose. He had been on the other side, on his knees, weeding a small garden.

"I'm Amos Poole—Admiral Amos Poole," he growled. "Charlie's father. Who are you?"

12

I do not recall what I mumbled to this flinty old sea dog. That first impression—the impression of an imaginative boy— was too overwhelming. The sight of him standing there, looming over me, staring down at me, was too busy being seared into my memory forever.

Amos Poole looked like no one I had ever known—all of whom were ordinary people made of flesh and bones. Instead, this towering figure calling itself "Amos Poole— Admiral Amos Poole" seemed to be made of knotted rope and deck planking. His tanned face was creased and folded like the ocean floor. His nose, chin and ears were larger than they should have been. All this was topped by icy white, close-cropped hair that looked like the polar cap astride the world. His sparkling green eyes inexplicably reminded me of mossy sea shells glistening on a sunlit rock, washed by the endless surf. He had anchor chains for fingers—broad, gnarled and rusty. Amos Poole, to my young lively mind, was an apparition born fully grown out of the abyssal depth of the briny sea. I had no reason to doubt that he was Neptune himself, ancient god of the ocean deep.

After that first meeting, Amos Poole and I gradually became good friends. At last he found someone to talk too—someone who would enjoy listening to his gripping dramas of the sea. Charlie paid little attention to him. I suppose he had heard it all too many times before. Come to think of it, I cannot remember seeing Charlie about the place whenever Amos and I were together. Anyway, I was an eager listener. The only barrier between us was the U. S. Government fence.

Amos told me of his adventures with Dewey at Manila Bay and of his world cruise with the Great White Fleet. There were tales of storms and wrecks; of sea monsters and distant ports. There was no end to Amos Poole's life on the high seas.

Mostly, however, he talked about the old days—"the real old

days," he used to say. The days of wooden ships, canvas and wind. "When men were men," he insisted. "When the greatest struggle on the boiling sea was the battle of Man and Whale—New England Man and Whale."

When Amos talked of whalemen, whaleboats and whales the stories always drifted to New England and his father, Jeremiah—one of the last of the weatherbeaten, leather-face New England sailors—according to Amos' reckoning—who made New Bedford their home port and whaling their life work.

As time went on I learned a few details about the Poole family. I learned that Jeremiah was born in Mystic, Connecticut, the first of the five children of Isaiah and Hannah Poole. Isaiah was the minister of the Mystic Seamen's Congregational Church. Jeremiah was soon joined by his four sisters—Rebecca, Sarah, Rachel and Miriam. Only Sarah eventually married and it was a childless marriage. And only Rachel and Sarah outlived their brother, Jeremiah. As for Jeremiah—he married Augusta Bartlett in 1852. He was twenty-five and master of his own ship at the time. Augusta was eighteen. I learned, too, that Augusta—Amos' mother—died in childbirth three years later. Amos was raised by his aunts Rebecca and Rachel until he entered the U. S. Naval Academy at Annapolis, Maryland. He married Martha Parker in 1880—the same day he graduated. Charlie, their only son who became keeper of the Norton's Point Light, was born eight years later. Charlie never married.

In any event, Amos talked mostly of his father's first sea voyage and the tragic circumstances that led him there at the age of fourteen. It was the very beginning of three generations of Pooles at sea and I suppose Amos was quite proud of the fact.

It seemed that Isaiah died suddenly in his pulpit a few days after Jeremiah had passed his twelfth birthday. As Amos told it—Isaiah's last words were from the final chapter of the Book of Revelation—"Surely, I come quickly," he was heard to whisper. And surely did he go quickly. He never spoke again. The good Lord was merciful to His faithful servant, but not to those left behind. Hannah Poole and her five children were left without a penny or any means of support. Hannah tried her best with small work but it was hardly enough. The girls were all too young to help and Jeremiah was unskilled at every useful trade. Jeremiah could read and write. His father saw to that. Jeremiah was being prepared for the ministry. But his literary skills were useless among a people who took their livelihood from the sea.

For two years Hannah struggled along, but the family's circumstances went from bad to worse. Finally, in 1841, she was forced to make an agreement that sent her son, Jeremiah, to sea to earn their fortune. Jeremiah protested. He feared and detested a life at sea. Hannah cried. But there was little else they could do.

Accordingly, Hannah signed a contract with Mr. Charles Lockwood, owner of the whaleship *Evening Star*—a contract that put Jeremiah aboard the ship as an apprentice—a ship's boy—for a voyage that would take him from home for at least three years. In return for these services, Jeremiah's "lay" of the ship's profits was set at $\frac{1}{200}$. If the venture proved to be successful, his share could amount to about $300.

It seemed that every time Amos and I met across that fence, bits and pieces of his father's first voyage came to the surface as if washed ashore like flotsam jarred loose from a long forgotten sunken wreck.

I never knew the entire story. There were dark hints of trouble and unpleasantness of every dimension. I did learn, however, that the *Evening Star* went down with all hands save one—Jeremiah Poole—he had left the ship somewhere

and later signed on another vessel—this time as an ordinary seaman. Whatever took place aboard the ill-fated *Evening Star* became the sole knowledge of one person—Jeremiah Poole. Apparently, and for reasons best known to himself, Jeremiah remained silent about it all the rest of his life.

But these tales came to an abrupt end shortly after America went to war in 1941. Charlie Poole retired from the United States Lighthouse Service and returned to New Bedford, Massachusetts. In 1946, a brief notice of the death of Admiral Amos Poole, USN retired, appeared in the New York *Times.* He was ninty-one years old.

While the passing years—about thirty of them—dimmed the glow of those summer days at the lighthouse fence, they were never able to erase the face and figure of Amos Poole from my mind. He was there, constantly. It was not until a very recent evening that the entire episode came vividly alive, once more.

My wife, three children and I returned to the old house in Sea Gate for a family visit. No sooner had we arrived when a violent storm fell out of the sky and lashed the area. The house shook. The sound and fury of the smashing surf mixed with driving rain and an assortment of thunderclaps was deafening. The lights nervously flickered off and on until they went out altogether. The rotating, flashing red beacon of the Norton's Point Lighthouse, nearby, cast a devilish beam into the living room as always. Now, without house lights, it seemed brighter. Within a few minutes, however, emergency candles burned in various parts of the house.

Somehow, above the sound of the storm, I heard the insistent ringing of the doorbell. Thinking it was the back, or leeward, door—since that was the only entrance used during the winter or bad weather—I raced for it and opened it. No one was there. I crossed the foyer and headed for the seaward door—the main entrance—wondering why anyone would be using it now. I reached the door, had some difficulty unlocking it, but finally flung it open.

Standing there, hatless and dripping, the pounding surf not fifty yards behind him, was a ghost newly risen from the bottom of that raging sea—Amos Poole! At least that is who I thought it was in the half light of a candle.

"You won't remember me," yelled the shadowy, sopping figure. "I'm Charlie Poole."

I remembered Charlie Poole, all right, but this was not Charlie Poole!

I drew back, staring at what I knew had to be the ghost of Amos Poole—Admiral Amos Poole—dead and buried twenty-five years before! I was not about to invite him in.

"I'm Charlie Poole," he yelled again. "I used to be the light-keeper," he added, pointing a knotty finger toward the flashing beacon. "I jes' came over to give you this," he bellowed over the crashing storm. "I found it over at the light and thought you'd be interested in having it considerin' how friendly you and my father used to be. I didn't expect to find you or the old family still here. But I took a chance and came over."

He shoved a package into my trembling hands. The package, a box wrapped in old brown bag paper tied together with a hairy string, was soaking wet.

He started to leave, hesitated, turned around and spoke again. "I jes' came down from New Bedford way to see the light once more."

A likely story I thought.

"She's a beauty, you know. She shor' is. There are no more

21

of us Pooles. I'm the last. Take care of them papers."

With that, Charlie Poole, Amos Poole's ghost or whoever he was, disappeared into the storm. For all I know he went back into the sea where he probably came from. I could believe anything at that point. I stood there, in the open doorway, quivering from head to toe. Finally, I shut the door, locked it and placed the package on a table.

"Who was that?" someone called out.

"No one," I answered, "just the wind and rain."

Quickly, I cut the string with a pocketknife and removed the wet wrapping. An old cardboard box lay exposed before me. I lifted the top. Inside was another bulky package. This was wrapped in oilskin. I removed it only to find three more separately wrapped packets—also covered with oilskin. I peeled the wrapping from one of the packets and uncovered an old, worn photograph of Amos Poole taken during one of his visits to the lighthouse.

"God in heaven," I whispered to myself, "it *was* him, it was Amos who had just been here."

My hands began to tremble again, although I do not think they ever stopped shaking from the minute I saw him. A few minutes later I picked up the second packet and took off its wrapping. More pictures. One, another old photograph; the other, a small painted portrait on wood of a young boy. Amos Poole again, I thought. But no, it could not be. The painted portrait was dated "1841" and scribbled on the back of the photograph were the initials "JP" and the date "1901." It was Jeremiah Poole, himself! There was no doubt about it. Yet, strangely enough, while the painted face was unfamiliar to me, the face in the photo was not. It was the same one that spoke to me in the doorway only a few minutes before!

24

Now, the pieces began to fit together—or so I thought. The resemblance between Jeremiah, Amos and Charlie—if it was indeed Charlie at the door—was uncanny. But the more I thought about it the more I was taken with the chilling idea that Charlie was Amos and Amos was Jeremiah; that it was Jeremiah who told me those sea stories; and that it was Jeremiah who delivered this package. There never was an Amos Poole. There never was a Charlie Poole. There never was a family named Poole. There was only Jeremiah.

Impossible? Maybe. But there was one more packet to open.

I removed the oilskin from the third bundle. To my astonishment I found myself staring at a very old and brittle title page of a manuscript that lay underneath. I read the faded script:

BEING A SECRET ACCOUNT OF MY
HAZARDOUS VOYAGE AT SEA ABOARD
THE WHALESHIP EVENING STAR

BEGUN THIS DAY OF SATURDAY
SEPTEMBER 11 AT MYSTIC CONNECTICUT
IN THE YEAR OF OUR LORD 1841

GOD BLESS MR. TYLER PRESIDENT OF
THESE UNITED STATES
GOD BLESS MR. LOCKWOOD MY BENEFACTOR
GOD BLESS MY POOR MOTHER
GOD BLESS MY SISTERS
GOD BLESS THIS SHIP
GOD BLESS ME

JEREMIAH POOLE

Here was the actual account of Jeremiah's first whaling cruise written in his own hand—parts of which I heard so often at the lighthouse fence so long ago. In my mounting excitement I quit thinking about ghosts. Yet, as I turn these events

26

Being A Secret Account of My
Hazardous Voyage At Sea Aboard
The Whaleship Evening Star

Begun This Day Of Saturday
September 11 At Mystic Connecticut
In The Year Of Our Lord 1841

God Bless Mr. Tyler President Of
These United States
God Bless Mr. Lockwood My Benefactor
God Bless My Poor Mother
God Bless My Sisters
God Bless This Ship
God Bless Me

Jeremiah Poole

over in my mind now, I am left with so many unanswered questions.

Why had this revealing package been so many years hidden and undiscovered in the Norton's Point Lighthouse—if indeed it was? Why did Charlie Poole—if that is really who he was—and he must have been past eighty—choose this stormy night to make an appearance with the package? It hardly seems likely that such an old person would make such a difficult and lonely trip from New Bedford, Massachusetts, to Sea Gate in Brooklyn, New York, just to take a last sentimental look at the lighthouse. And how did he know so quickly when I opened the door that I, now grown to manhood, was the boy befriended by his late father? It never occurred to me that Charlie knew where I lived! And why make me the heir of such a possession—a manuscript that belongs in some historical collection—the only heirloom of a family that hardly exists—if it ever did to begin with?

I shiver as I try to unravel the mystery despite the fact that I know there must be a logical explanation. I grow cold, too, when I recall that dripping figure standing in the doorway of the old house in Sea Gate with the frightening sea and wild storm at his back. Who was to say he did not come from the ocean bottom? I was the only one to see him, to talk to him—or rather to hear him—he did the talking, not me. And I alone received the package and examined its contents. No one in that house saw me during those terrifying moments. I told no one about the pictures and manuscript—that is, not until now.

In recent days, I have tried to uncover additional information regarding several aspects of this tale. I have not been very successful. What little I have uncovered is so extraordinary that I hesitate to continue the search lest my curiosity turns from its present commonplace confusion to an everlasting

28

fear of the unknown. But more about this later.

Meanwhile, what follows is the manuscript—fourteen-year-old Jeremiah Poole's own story—told by himself. It is the story of a ship's boy aboard a whaler in the days when "men were men . . . when the greatest struggle on the boiling sea was the battle of man and whale—New England man and whale." It is the story of loneliness, labor, mayhem, murder and merrymaking as thirty-three men and a boy pursue the richest prize of that day—whale oil. It is a story of human survival—unknown for 130 years—a story in which men claimed their prize for a brief time until the sea claimed them all—forever.

PART II
JEREMIAH POOLE'S OWN ACCOUNT

Saturday, September 11, 1841

I do not know the hour. It has been dark for some time now. It makes no difference in this hot hole. It will be as black in the morning. My only light is a small candle. I have no air. The stink in here—grease, rum, fish, pitch—is choking the life out of me. I shall die before sunrise. Oh, God! I have no spirit for this! I am a victim of such misfortune!

I came aboard this afternoon. Mr. Hutchinson, ship's master, and Mr. Dixwell, first officer, stood at the head of the gangway. They said not one word to me other than to tell me who they were. Mr. Dixwell passed me on to a fellow he addressed as "Cockeye"—and that he is—one eye goes one way and the other eye goes another. His true name is Mr. Corley. He is a cooper. Cockeye showed me to my quarters, this small, rotten-smelling place. There is not enough room for a rat. At least I shall be alone. I am in a locker below the galley house in the aft end. The captain's cabin is nearby.

Cockeye took me on a walk to show me the ship's parts. I am as ignorant of this vessel now as I was before. I could not tell what he was looking at. I did not much care. I hear music through the timbers. It is far off. No one seems to be about. The only other sounds are the creaks of the ship and the lapping water below.

The galley is locked. But I brought along some biscuits. I ate these for my supper. I thought I would remain outside this night. It is warm enough and the air is sweeter above. But I dare not—not now. Already I have seen a dreadful sight and we are not yet under way. The ship is still tied to the wharf and I to my grieving mother.

Not a moment ago I saw two men dragging a third toward

a hatch. Another, who I am sure was Mr. Goodspeed—he came along with Mr. Lockwood to see my mother about these arrangements—was beating the victim. The man was very still. They dropped him down the hatch. They did not see me. I shall be very quiet now while I find a proper hiding place for these papers. No one needs to know of my scribbling pleasures.

Sunday, September 12, 1841

Eight Bells. It is midnight. We are dead in the water—midstream in the river. We were towed out here at noon.

There were many visitors aboard this morning. Most of the crew seemed to be here. Some rowed out later. There was much coming and going. No one paid attention to me. I had no visitors. It is just as well. I do not think I could have suffered another farewell with my dear mother.

I helped some of the crew settle in their quarters. They all seemed to be decent fellows. Mr. Goodspeed tried to kick me once. I do not know why. But he was too drunk and missed his mark. I shall have to be careful of him. Mr. Dixwell observed the scene. He said something to Mr. Goodspeed and then ordered me to the galley to help Mr. Harrigan, the cook. Mr. Harrigan does not have a single tooth in his head. He came down with the scurvy once and they all fell out. Everyone calls him "Gummy."

A short prayer meeting was held before the ship broke from the wharf. Most of the visitors departed with the final "amen." Some remained on board during the tow. These had been in the captain's cabin all afternoon merrymaking. One of them staggered out and walked off the ship. He nearly drowned. Mr. Hansen, second officer, was on the ladder coming aboard when it happened. He

34

jumped in after him. They were both fished out but the man quickly fell in again. They got him out and tied him to a rail.

I saw nothing of the man being dragged and beaten last night. He has not left this ship. I am certain of that. God have mercy on him whoever he is.

All remaining visitors were rowed ashore at nine o'clock this evening. The whaleboat returned and was hoisted aboard. Now we are alone and waiting. The night is clear, warm and breezy.

Monday, September 13, 1841

We are at sea. All ties are broken. The land is gone. I am gone. Oh, my poor mother. I shall not see her again.

Tuesday, September 14, 1841

The sea is calm these twenty-four hours.

I was everywhere today. Do this, boy—do that, boy—over here, boy—over there, boy—step lively, boy—look alive, boy. I am sore with aches and bruises. I helped Gummy for a time in the galley. Afterward, Mr. Starkweather, a boatsteerer, had me stow his lances and irons in a whaleboat. Mr. Curtis and Mr. Milton, boatsteerers, too, stowed their own harpoons. I did some errands for Mr. Franklin, the blacksmith, and Irish O'Brien, ship's carpenter. Once Mr. Hutchinson inquired after my well-being, but he walked quickly by before I could answer him. There was much activity.

Wednesday, September 15, 1841

The sea is rolling as is this ship. There has been a light rain. Everything is damp and sticky. I do not feel well. Mostly I am frightened. I was below somewhere when I became confused as to which direction I was headed. I heard some voices. I saw some figures. I was about to seek their aid—to be pointed aright—when all at once I could not. Someone in the shadows behind me clapped a huge hand over my mouth and held me fast. At that moment I saw the figures more clearly. There—on his knees—was the man I saw on that first night being dragged and beaten. Above him stood Mr. Goodspeed and the captain Mr. Hutchinson! Suddenly, Mr. Goodspeed kicked the wretched man still. He and the captain departed. Whereupon the hand dropped from my mouth and I came face to face with a large black man who quickly told me he was Ezra January and that I was to follow him. I did. We got the poor beaten man into the crew's quarters nearby where I discovered that he was known to me—a traveling peddler who came through Mystic every summer. He was known only as "Buttons" owing to his trade—he sold brass buttons. No one knew his true name or where he came from. Mr. January sent me off to my locker with a word not to speak of these events to anyone. I told no one of what I saw now or before.

Thursday, September 16, 1841

I have not eaten. I am unable to. The weather is foul. The sea heaves. I heave. There is little activity. I am more ill than I know. My end is near.

Friday, September 17, 1841

Calm the waters, dear Lord. Calm this ship, dear Lord. I am sick and finished. I pray for my salvation. Help me, please, dear Lord.

Sunday, September 19, 1841

I have been heard. The sea has improved. I am better.

EVENING STAR
MYSTIC CONNECTICUT

The ship is steady. The captain held a service today. He thanked God for our deliverance. There was no work today—it being the Sabbath. I did clean up the galley, however.

Buttons was at the service. He looked gray and distant. His face is bruised. His enemies are powerful here.

Monday, September 20, 1841

Eight days at sea. I am too far from all I love and going farther. Our heading has been due east these twenty-four hours. The wind is fair and warm. The sea is very blue. Two boats were lowered into the water this morning. Mr. Hansen and Mr. Goodspeed each took a crew of six to practice. Mr. Dixwell took his six in the afternoon. The labors have been well planned out. There are the officers who have their stations and particular duties. There are the shipkeepers—the coopers, blacksmith, carpenter, cook and me. We are expected to handle the ship while the mast hands—the rest of the crew—are hunting, killing, cutting and boiling the beasts—the great whales.

Tuesday, September 21, 1841

Our heading is still due east. We are running very smoothly. The breeze is stiff and warm. Gummy tells me that we are on the northern edge of the Gulf Stream south of the Grand Banks.

Thursday, September 23, 1841

I was too tired to make an entry last night. I am less tired now. When I am not in the galley I am with Mr. Franklin and his hot irons or with Cockeye and another cooper, Mr. Henry Clarke. Cockeye says we are going to need all these barrels for our treasure. He means whale oil.

I saw Buttons in the rigging. He is much afraid up there.

40

He almost fell to his certain death yesterday. He caught his foot in a line and dangled in the air upside down— screaming. Some of the mast hands came to him, put a line around him, freed his foot and lowered him to the deck. Mr. Goodspeed laughed and sent him back up. Several of the men protested this. It did no good.

Sunday, September 26, 1841

I have been fourteen days at sea now. Our heading is more northerly. The wind is brisk. The sea is still flat but not as blue. We are running very fast. Gummy says that we are going for a cooler climate to the northeast of the Banks where the hunting is good.

There was the usual Sabbath service this morning after which I found a windless place in the sun. Ezra January came over. He is a landsman like me. He has never been to sea before. He said that he was a runaway slave up from the Carolinas and that Mr. Lockwood let him come aboard to escape his pursuers.

Mr. Dixwell came by. He is a friendly sort. The men like him. But he does not seem to be as thick with the captain as he should be. Mr. Goodspeed acts more like the first officer. Mr. Dixwell talked to us about the ship and its workings and what to expect when we sight our first whale.

The *Evening Star* is a sturdy ship in every particular. She is two years old and met with every success on her first run. This is her second run. She is a square-rigged bark of 311 tons. She is 103 feet along her main deck fore to aft; $25\frac{1}{2}$ feet in the beam. She draws $15\frac{1}{2}$ feet of water. There are several whaleboats hung from davits along the port side. There is a boat on the starboard bow and two others on the starboard quarter. Forward of the main hatch, which is dead amidships, is a bench used by Irish

41

O'Brien, ship's carpenter. Here, too, Cockeye and Mr. Clarke make barrels. Between the bench and the forehatch are the tryworks. These are two great iron pots in a brick furnace. A brick chimney rises through a wood roof that covers the tryworks from starboard to port. The furnace is set in a low pan filled with sea water called the "goose pen." Mr. Dixwell says that this keeps the furnace flame from setting the ship afire. Here, in the tryworks, pieces of whale called "bible leaves" are boiled for the oil.

Behind the main hatch is the main mast and the booby hatch. There are several spare whaleboats lashed to the deck on both sides of the hatch. Overhead is another roof. Farther on is the mizzen mast. Directly behind the mizzen is the great cabin skylight and the ship's wheel. The wheel is covered by a short roof that connects some lockers on the port side and the galley house on the starboard. The whole of this shed is called the "hurricane house."

Mr. Dixwell began to tell us about the "cutting-in stage," a wood platform suspended above the starboard gangway amidships. But he was called away.

Thursday, September 30, 1841

It is very cold these twenty-four hours. Sky and sea are without color. Lookouts have been aloft all week. Mr. Hutchinson paces and watches the horizon for any sign. All we have seen are several sharks in our wake feasting on Gummy's garbage.

Friday, October 1, 1841

Mr. Hutchinson grows impatient. His temper is short. The men complain about his quickness. They do not like Mr. Goodspeed's temper either. But he has been foul since the beginning. No one likes him. Nearly every hand is in fear

of him. He has taken to wearing a pistol.

I worked with Mr. Starkweather today. He is a pleasant man. It is still a mystery to me why the ship's harpoonists—we have five, three firsts, two seconds—are called boatsteerers. Mr. Starkweather told me to keep an eye out at the first kill and I shall know.

We made the gear in the whaleboats secure and ready. These boats are all of a kind—long and narrow—loaded to the gunnels. There is all manner of irons stowed away. Some have a single point which I learn are called "flues." They look like half an arrow. Some have two flues. These look like iron arrows. There are certain irons called "toggles." These have several sharply pointed curved flues on one side. There are dozens of lances and a number of irons with broad, flat sharp ends called "spades." There are two tubs of line stowed at the bow of each boat. One line runs from a tub over the oarlocks on one side around a post at the stern and returns to the bow over the oars on the other side. At the bow the line is secured to a harpoon. Also, there are a mast and sail stowed away in each boat.

Saturday, October 2, 1841

Nothing but sharks. We are now nineteen days at sea.

Sunday, October 3, 1841

The devil has boarded this ship!

We had our service. Afterward, Mr. Hutchinson ordered Mr. Goodspeed to have a boat lowered. The captain wanted more practice. Mr. Goodspeed made some of the green hands to stand by. There was Ezra January and John Drummer, the two landsmen; Buttons; Mr. Long,

46

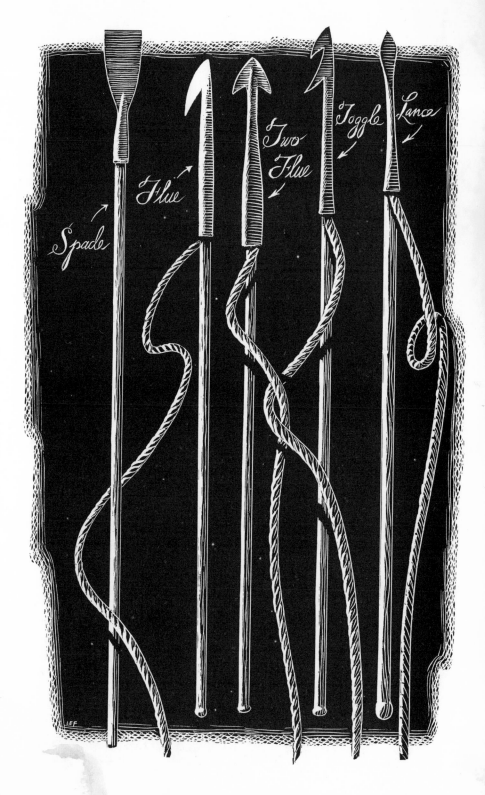

Spade

Flue

Two Flue

Toggle

Lance

ordinary seaman, Mat Farmer, seaman; and Mr. Cook, second boatsteerer.

Mr. Cook, speaking for all, refused to get into the boat. It was the Sabbath he said. Mr. Dixwell favored the men saying that it was not necessary to practice in a treacherous sea. And that it was! The sea came at us with terrible strength. It still does. We dip and buck and shiver from stem to stern. There was much shouting. Mr. Hutchinson watched from the wheel and said nothing, leaving Mr. Goodspeed to carry out his order. No one moved. Finally, Mr. Goodspeed picked up Buttons—a small man—and threw him into the boat. Mat Farmer and Ezra January, seeing this, became enraged. Mr. Hansen pushed Mr. Goodspeed, and Mr. Dixwell protested to the captain. But Mr. Farmer suddenly struck Mr. Goodspeed a deserving blow that sent him crashing into some kettles at the tryworks. There Ezra jumped on him and beat him further. Mr. Hansen pulled him off only to have Mat Farmer continue the beating. Mr. Hansen and some others then tried to pull them apart and nearly succeeded when Mr. Goodspeed loosened his pistol and fired a shot into Mat Farmer's heart. He died then and there. "Mutiny," cried Mr. Goodspeed. "Mutiny!" "Murder," cried the rest. "Murder!"

Someone kicked Mr. Goodspeed's pistol free and several hands dragged him to the captain. The captain was like stone. He said that there would be no practice; that he would decide about mutiny and the courts would decide about murder; that he would record these events as an eyewitness; that Mr. Goodspeed was following his orders; that Mat Farmer and Ezra should not have acted so rashly but that Mr. Goodspeed should not have used his pistol; and that he was truly sorry about what happened

to Mat Farmer. He continued Mr. Goodspeed as third officer and had Ezra clapped in irons below. Afterward, a service was held for the soul of Mat Farmer and he was buried in the wild sea.

Now there is much anger and sullenness among the crew. Mr. Dixwell told the men that we shall have justice but not mutiny; that whales are our business and that we should get on with this business or else we shall all return home poor men. Still, there is much grumbling.

Monday, October 4, 1841

Yesterday is forgotten today. Hardly had the first light of morning showed in the east when I heard the lookouts.

"Blow-ow, blow-ow, thar she blows!"

And there they were—several whales blowing and steaming not too far off our starboard beam. The creatures seemed to be swimming along with us. No boats were lowered at first. The officers and boatsteerers watched them very carefully. Later I learned that they were figuring how long the whales stayed on the surface before sounding for food; and then how long they stayed down before surfacing again. They were also figuring the whales' course and where they came up after sounding. Meanwhile, all sail was shortened. The crews were in the boats but not in the water. Soon enough, one of the whales sounded and the three port boats were lowered. The *Evening Star* had come about so that the whales were on our port side.

The boatmen pulled hardily on their oars and quickly reached a place. They separated somewhat and waited. The sea rolled gently—unlike yesterday. There was a slight mist but I could see them clearly. I kept an eye on Mr. Dixwell's boat—especially Mr. Starkweather.

50

Suddenly the water broke and a great black creature with a great square head and large tail appeared near Mr. Dixwell's boat. Mr. Starkweather got up from his station at one of the bow oars; Mr. Jones had the other bow oar. He took hold of the iron secured to the line, stood up in the bow with a knee hard against a post and guided the boat—Mr. Dixwell was at the stern steering oar—closer to the beast. The whale did not seem to know that the boat was coming up on it. Swiftly then, Mr. Starkweather hurled the iron into the creature. Swiftly, too, the boat backed off with much line showing between the stuck harpoon and the boat.

The whale began to beat the water with its flukes sending great showers of sea water into the boat. I noticed that Mr. Starkweather had changed stations with Mr. Dixwell. Mr. Starkweather was now steering the boat and Mr. Dixwell held a lance with his knee in the bow post. I suppose this is why Mr. Starkweather and the others are called boatsteerers. I shall have to inquire again.

As I thought the beast to be now dead I began to turn away when a great shout split the air. Hardly dead and bleeding little, the whale began to swim with uncommon speed, knocking Mr. Dixwell backward into the boat, his lance falling into the water. It swam in a great arc around the ship dragging Mr. Dixwell's boat. The other two boats seemed well out of the way. Everyone began shouting. Mr. Hutchinson's voice was the loudest. He was in the rigging holding on with one hand and waving his cap with the other. The rest of us ran from one side to the other and back again to see the action. Gummy said it was the best Nantucket sleigh ride he had ever seen.

Presently the whale stopped. The boat pulled up alongside and Mr. Dixwell sunk another lance deep inside the rolling hulk. He did this several times until a great fountain of

51

blood spouted from the whale's head. Again the boat backed off as the beast began to thrash the water. It shook its huge body and smacked the sea with its great flukes with such force that the water all around was turned into a boiling bloody bath. The sea turned deep red. Finally, the whale rolled over. It was dead. The boat approached once more. Mr. Dixwell made certain of the kill by plunging a lance into the creature's eye. The dead whale was towed to the starboard and lashed to the ship.

Mr. Hansen's boat took another whale in the very same manner. Now there are two great beasts tied alongside. Night came too quickly for further work. There is a better mood now.

Tuesday, October 5, 1841

The two whales are still tied to us. Mr. Hutchinson hoped to kill another before cutting them up. But not through a day of watchfulness were any more to be seen. The days are very short in these northern latitudes. I trust that Mr. Hutchinson will soon change our course southward. I hear that we shall call at the Azores for provisions.

I went to see Ezra. The poor man is chained to a post. He was sick and hungry. I tried to bring him some food— some salt pork stew—but Mr. Goodspeed blocked my path. He asked me where I was going. I told him. He knocked the bowl out of my hand. It spilled all over the deck. He made me clean it up and struck me several blows as I did so. Mr. Dixwell happened upon the scene. He spun Mr. Goodspeed around and slammed him against the rail. The two of them almost went over the side. A crowd gathered behind Mr. Dixwell facing Mr. Goodspeed, whose back was to the sea. The captain came over. A good thing he did, too. In another minute the men would have thrown

Mr. Goodspeed into the water. The captain managed to prevent this and sent the men back to their stations. But Mr. Dixwell would not be put off. He protested Mr. Goodspeed's behavior since putting to sea and hoped the captain would consider the interest and well-being of his men with respect to a successful voyage. Finally, he told Mr. Goodspeed that he had not one ounce of Christian charity in his blood and warned him to mend his ways from that moment on or he would be a dead mate. Mr. Hutchinson then warned Mr. Goodspeed to act as a proper officer in the interest of the cruise and bade the two men to kill the whale and not each other. He then sent me off for another bowl of stew. I brought this to Ezra who was grateful.

Later, Buttons came over. It was his first opportunity to thank Ezra for what he had done on his account Sunday last. Buttons told us how he was forced into his present circumstances. He had been doing business in Mystic. Among those to whom he had sold some buttons and other sundries were the captain and Mr. Goodspeed. Late that same night he took to the road to be at his next place by dawn. He was accosted by some men in the darkness. They were drunk. He recognized Mr. Goodspeed but not the others. Mr. Goodspeed said that he and the captain had been cheated. Buttons swore that he was an honest man and that they were mistaken. Mr. Goodspeed thought otherwise and said that Buttons would pay dearly for his lying as well as his cheating. Whereupon they smashed his goods; stole his money; knocked him down and carried him off. There were no witnesses—of that he was certain.

"I shall not see a dollar from all this," he cried. "They will kill me in the end. I shall disappear and none shall be the wiser. They do not even carry my name on the ship's papers. Unless I am spoken for there will never be

56

proof of my presence on this ship. Mr. Hutchinson is part of this unholy conspiracy. He is amused by the crime. The villagers will think I was lost in the forests. No one knows I am here. I have no family, no friends, no residence."

Ezra told us his situation was worse. He had been a slave. He thought he was free in New England. But now here he was chained like a dog to a post.

Ezra said no more. But Buttons said that he would drive a knife into Mr. Goodspeed's evil heart before he met his Maker. They cautioned me to keep silent or else I would meet a cruel fate—in the jaws of a shark—like Gummy's garbage.

I do not know at whose hands I will suffer this fate. Theirs—Buttons and Ezra's—or Mr. Goodspeed's. There is murder in the air and I am in the middle. Mr. Dixwell means me no harm and there are others who are well meaning toward me. But I shall trust in the goodness of the Lord. He shall watch over me—Buttons and Ezra too. They are victims of unspeakable cruelty.

Wednesday, October 6, 1841

They cut the whales today. Oh, God, what a bloody sight!

I had become accustomed to their presence since Monday—lashed to us, as they were, with heavy chains—their great square heads to our stern. Cockeye said they had been there too long and that work should have begun on them soon after the kill. But I cannot say that I see how it mattered. The beasts are no more, now.

Work began at first light this morning. All of the tools—spades, knives, all manner of blades and hooks were arranged in a row on deck. A wood platform—the cutting-in stage—was swung out over the side and made fast above

58

the nearest carcass. All of the ship's officers—Mr. Hutch-inson, Mr. Dixwell, Mr. Hansen, Mr. Goodspeed—went out onto the platform with their blades. The sea was choppy and running before a cold, quick wind. There was a steep and steady roll to the ship. The salty spray stung my face and drenched the men on the platform.

Mr. Hutchinson directed his officers to tie themselves to the platform railing to keep from getting knocked into the water. He did the same. Meanwhile, he observed that the whale directly below was not in a proper position. He ordered the carcass to be rolled on its side so that its belly and jaw were secured against the hull.

This done, Mr. Hutchinson began to cut into the whale near its jaw, slicing here and slicing there. The others on the cutting-in stage made no move to assist. All they did was watch. "The first cut belongs to the captain," someone told me. "It is the custom." Soon Mr. Moses Cummings, seaman, was lowered onto the slippery whale where he quickly inserted a hook into the loosened blubber. The hook was attached to a line connected to a hauling ma-chine, the windlass. After Mr. Cummings was hoisted aboard, some of the crew began to turn the windlass which pulled on the line causing the blubber to peel away from the whale. The peeled blubber is called the "blanket."

As the men heaved away on the windlass and peeled the blanket, the whale slowly rolled until its belly and jaw faced the open sea.

Now the captain and all the officers began to slice more of the blanket and finally removed the narrow strip which was hauled aboard. A chain was passed around the whale's jaw. More and deeper cuts were made behind the jaw at the animal's throat. Presently, the long jaw was made loose, wrenched free and hauled on deck. The whale was

then rolled from side to side so that lines and chains could be passed through the great head. When these lines were secured, the four men on the stage made a huge ugly cut that went deep inside the whale—to its backbone. There they jabbed furiously at the bone until it parted. The deck hands then heaved on the lines and chains until they tore the animal's head from its body. The head was not put aboard. Instead, it was secured to the aft end.

I shall have to continue this account at my next opportunity. My candle is nearly gone. I am weary.

Sunday, October 10, 1841

Twenty-eight days at sea.

I did not think that my next opportunity for continuing this account would be so many days hence. There has been much to do. I have a new candle—thanks to Gummy.

Following the severing of the whale's head, the carcass was rolled over and over and over until all the strips of blanket—the blubber—were removed and hoisted aboard. All that remained were the flukes and the headless, peeled carcass. This was cast adrift. The head was then brought back to the cutting-in stage. It was too heavy to be hoisted aboard all at once. It was cut into two parts, each part hauled up separately. One of the parts looked to be all blubber. The other part had some waxy white stuff called "spermaceti." I did not learn until the following day that both whales were "sperm whales."

The blubber blankets which had been hoisted aboard were kept below—deep in the bowels of the ship—in the "blubber room." There the blankets were cut into pieces called "horse pieces." These horse pieces were brought to the tryworks on deck, cut into smaller sections, or "bible

leaves," with mincing knives and thrown into the iron furnace pots where they were boiled. The boiled leaves gave up the "treasure"—the sperm oil. The hot oil was pailed out of the cooking pots and spilled into some copper vessels nearby where it was allowed to cool. After it had cooled enough it was again pailed out and poured into wood barrels lashed to the railings. From these barrels the oil passed through canvas hoses to fresh barrels in the ship's hold where it was stowed. The boiled-out scrap was removed from the cooking pots and fed to the trywork fire for fuel.

The crew then dealt with the whale's head. The first section was cut into pieces and boiled out. The second section was sliced open. The spermaceti—the white, waxy stuff inside—was scooped out. There was so much of it that it formed a thickness up to my chest. All of this was put into the tryworks pots, heated up to a liquid, cooled, pailed into barrels and stowed away.

The second whale was disposed of in the same manner as the first.

The work went on all through the night; half of the crew working topside, the other half toiling below. The furnace sent up heavy black clouds that coated the entire ship— from stem to stern—with a thick, greasy rotten-smelling soot. The whole of the *Evening Star* looked in the light of day as if it had been charred, seared and roasted in a fatty fire. The decks were awash with a filthy, oily slippery ooze that sloshed from starboard to port with every roll of the ship. It was deep enough in places to come above my boot tops. Some of the slime found its way below—slowly dripping through the weakest joints in the deck planking or splashing through a hatchway or descending a gangway ladder. The whole of me was soak-

ing in this misery. The stink from it all settled on me like a hellish, sickening mantle. I wanted to tear off my clothes and fling myself into the clean sea. But for the sake of my widowed mother I remained aboard and suffered until Friday noon. It was then that we were overcome by a squall and cleansed by the fresh rain and wind until sunup yesterday morning. God can be merciful and forgiving!

Sunday, October 17, 1841

Thirty-five days at sea.

We have been cruising these northern waters for a week—north, south, east and west. We have seen nothing. All is peaceful. Mr. Goodspeed sulks about but otherwise creates no mischief.

There are two brothers on the *Evening Star*—Rob and Johnnie Bristol. I knew them back in Mystic although they did not frequent my father's Sunday services. They are not much older than I am but they have been to sea before. Johnnie, who is the older one, is a most artistic fellow. He came aboard with a violin and scratched out a tune from time to time. But now his violin is silent. It swelled so badly in the dampness that it split in several places.

This afternoon Johnnie painted my likeness on a piece of wood. He found some colors and brushes in the paint locker. He made me very red in the face but everyone says it is a remarkable likeness. I have put it away for safe-keeping.

Wednesday, October 20, 1841

Thirty-eight days.

Our heading has been southeast these twenty-four hours.

66

Thursday, October 21, 1841

Ezra suffers terribly. He has been in irons these past two
weeks or more. I have managed to visit with him each
day as have Buttons, Mr. Dixwell, and Mr. Hansen and
several others. Ezra told me that Mr. Dixwell is trying
to secure his release but the captain keeps putting him
off. Ezra is still hopeful that Mr. Dixwell will succeed.
I hope he will too. Ezra is a good man.

Saturday, October 23, 1841

There is trouble again! Mr. Goodspeed is at the bottom
of it—damn his evil heart! Buttons is gone—gone and
done with. Lord have mercy on his poor soul.

I saw it happen; so did Mr. Pedro Rua, the Portuguee.
It was late this morning. There was a goodly mist. I was
helping Mr. Rua secure a line up forward that had come
loose during the night. Mr. Rua and I were going about
the work in silence when presently we saw Mr. Goodspeed
come out of the mist pushing the protesting Buttons before him. Neither of them saw us—most assuredly not Mr.
Goodspeed. If he had, he never would have done what
suddenly came next right before our horrified eyes. God!
What an evil deed!

Mr. Goodspeed pushed Buttons toward the rail—God only
knows why. As Buttons stumbled and slipped trying to
get away, Mr. Goodspeed tripped him and Buttons went
over the side. It happened so fast there was little we could
do. Mr. Goodspeed then walked quickly aft and disappeared down deck through the mist which now seemed
thicker than moments before. Mr. Rua and I rushed to
the rail. We heard nothing—not a sound except the com-
mon shipboard noises—the rushing wind, flapping canvas,
creaks and groans and hissing sea. We saw nothing but

the fog, not even the water.

Mr. Rua and I went forthwith to Mr. Dixwell. We told him what we saw. He told us to keep silent. "Who would believe such a wild tale from the mouth of a babe," he said. "Who would believe such a wild tale from the mouth of a Portuguee."

Mr. Rua became so angry that he cursed Mr. Dixwell in a flood of words that none of us understood. But Mr. Dixwell tried to calm him explaining that if we did make our witness known we would be dead, too, sooner or later.

Mr. Rua became even more angry. He grabbed me by the arm and before I knew it we were in the captain's cabin. Mr. Dixwell came after us but did not enter the cabin. Mr. Rua told the captain what had happened. Mr. Hutchinson laughed and said we were crazy. "Who is Buttons?" he asked. We tried to tell him again. "No one by that name has ever been aboard this vessel," he said. With that, he shoved a list in front of us. There were thirty-three names on it—names of every member of the crew and officers. There was a line drawn through Mat Farmer's name— accompanied by the note "died at sea." Everyone was accounted for. There was no listing for Buttons. "Show me your Buttons," he said. "You have sea fever," he continued and sent us away.

Mr. Rua returned to his station. I went back to my locker not knowing what to do or what would happen next. I decided to quit the privacy of my quarters and remain the rest of the voyage with the crew. It would be safer that way. As I came out of my locker I heard voices coming from the captain's cabin, nearby. It was Mr. Goodspeed in there with the captain. They were arguing.

I heard Mr. Goodspeed say that he was glad to be rid of

that cheating peddler. I heard Mr. Hutchinson tell Mr. Goodspeed that his murderous deed was seen by me and Pedro Rua. Mr. Goodspeed then told the captain that he will rid himself of those "prying eyes." He told the captain not to interfere and that if he did stand in his way, he, Goodspeed, third mate, would inform Mr. Lockwood, ship's owner, that his captain, Hutchinson, used the *Evening Star*'s first voyage for considerable personal profit. It seemed that on that first voyage, Mr. Hutchinson ran a cargo of rifles—secretly—to Savannah, Georgia, where he sold them to the highest bidder for use in the Florida Seminole War.

"If Lockwood discovers your deception," said Mr. Goodspeed to the captain, "you will never again sail from a New England port as a ship's master."

I had heard enough. There was more to fear now than ever. I went to see Mr. Dixwell again. I told him what I had heard. Mr. Dixwell was alarmed. He had Mr. Hansen call Mr. Goodspeed into the rigging to occupy his attention. He had Mr. Starkweather accompany him to the captain's cabin and bade him to wait outside the door and so prevent anyone's entry. I followed and waited with Mr. Starkweather before the door while Mr. Dixwell and the captain had words.

There we heard Mr. Dixwell and Mr. Hutchinson strike a bargain. They intend to rid themselves and this ship of Mr. Goodspeed. We heard Mr. Dixwell tell the captain that he was not interested in his previous gun traffic and knew nothing about it until this day; that all he was interested in was whale oil and a safe voyage and was not about to have a madman put him off. For his part, the captain would be happy to be rid of Mr. Goodspeed, if for no other reason, than to be free to run his ship in a

proper manner; and be free of a blackmailer forever.

Mr. Goodspeed's fate is sealed. He is going to die. I do not know how or when—I do not care to know. "It will be an accident," they said. God Almighty! What manner of men are these?

"You heard not a word," said Mr. Starkweather to me. "Stay clear and you shall reach a safe harbor."

God help me—please! I am going to be sick.

Sunday, October 24, 1841

Forty-two days. Mr. Goodspeed is still alive. Mr. Dixwell has me at his side all day.

Tuesday, October 26, 1841

All is quiet. It is too quiet. We have been running steadily southward. The air is warmer but I am still cold from the terror that awaits us all.

Wednesday, October 27, 1841

Mr. Goodspeed has perished! And glory be—he was smitten by the hand of the Lord and no one else. Justice has been served! Now Buttons and Mat Farmer can sleep in the deep in peace. But I weep for the boat crew that went down with Mr. Goodspeed. Why were they taken too? Who am I to question the Almighty? He has done in our tormentor and He has prevented Mr. Dixwell and the captain from committing an unspeakable crime. Ezra is free too! The captain has seen to that!

About noon today, Pedro Rua who was doing his watch in the nest, spotted five or six whales dead ahead.

"Blow-ow, blow-ow, dead ahead," he screamed.

The ship came alive. The boats were swung out. The beasts sounded. We timed them. They sounded again. We times them again. Now they came up not far astern to the starboard. The boats were lowered away. Mr. Goodspeed's boat broke out a sail and raced over the choppy sea to a point better than a mile behind us. We continued to tack with shortened sail but had every boat in sight.

Without warning and as Mr. Goodspeed's No. 3 boat lay in wait, a huge whale broke the surface in a great leap directly under the boat. Mr. Goodspeed, his crew and the boat were flung sky high in every direction. The boat came down right side up and we could see two or three men swimming toward it and finally reaching it. But it did them no good. The whale lashed at the boat with its flukes, missed and swamped the boat. It began to settle. But before it sank altogether, the beast swung around, clamped the boat in its jaws—as if it was a toy—snapped it in two and sounded. In an instant the boat—cut in half as it was—began to break up leaving hundreds of smaller pieces of wood and gear bobbing up and down on the rolling, choppy sea. We could not tell whether or not any of the crew—still living—was among the flotsam.

After a while, the No. 1 boat with Mr. Dixwell and the No. 2 boat with Mr. Hansen reached the area. They searched here and there but found no one. They were all lost—seven men—Mr. Goodspeed; Mr. William Milton, boatsteerer; Mr. Andrew Smithson, second boatsteerer; Edward Rose and Solomon Turner, seamen; Richard Welles and John Montgomerey, ordinary seamen both. May God have mercy on their souls—even Mr. Goodspeed's soul.

Mr. Hutchinson got out his speaking horn and ordered the two boats to return but they were on their way back anyway. Neither Mr. Dixwell nor Mr. Hansen were anxious to remain too long in that place and risk meeting a like fate—sent into eternity by a mad whale. The boats returned. The crews came aboard. Yet, Mr. Hutchinson was not satisfied. He brought the *Evening Star* around and cruised about the drifting remains of No. 3 boat looking for life. There was none. Night came and the ship turned south.

Thursday, October 28, 1841

Sometime during the previous night the *Evening Star* shivered from a dull thud that seemed to come from deep below. Everyone felt it and came on deck. It was too dark to see anything. Mr. Hutchinson ordered all hands below to seek out the cause. Nothing was found. All agreed that the mad whale had tried to upend the *Evening Star* and failing to do so would go away and not return. But we were wrong. A second thud came as I was halfway down the aft gangway. The ship lurched sideways and I nearly tumbled down the steps.

The captain sent parties below again to discover any damage. None was found. This time the creature went away. There was no further thudding.

During the morning a meeting was held. All hands assembled. The captain announced that a memorial prayer would be said for all of our lost hands on Sunday next.

The remainder of the meeting was taken up with our present situation. We have been at sea forty-six days. We have had two whales. We are shorthanded, having lost eight men—he never counted Buttons or even mentioned him—Buttons made nine lost—"Eight out of thirty-three listed," was what he said. We are in need of fresh vegetables, lemons and other fruits. "We are in need of a better

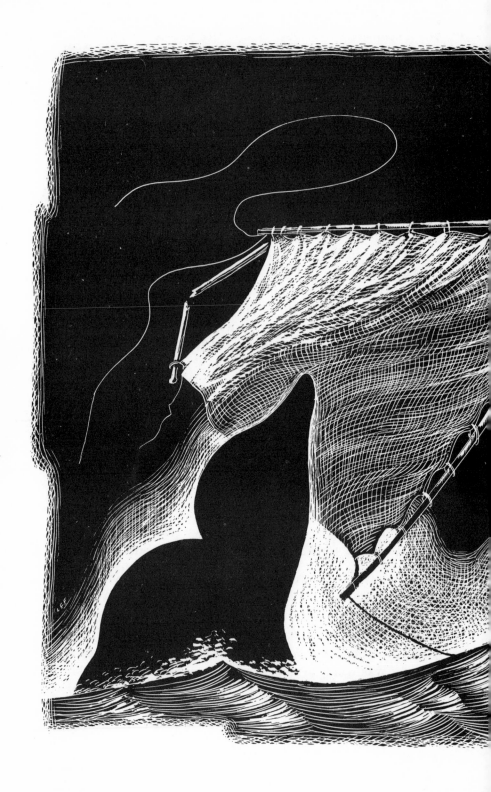

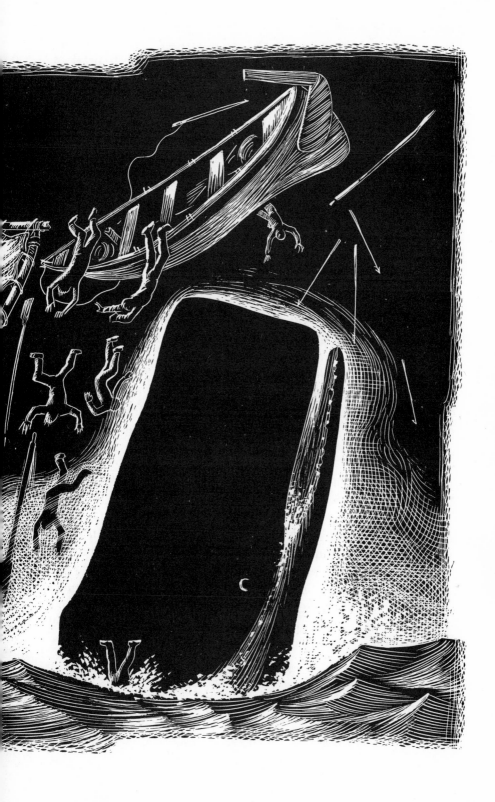

mood aboard this vessel," he said. "We are in need of relaxation and a new start," were his very words.

Mr. Hutchinson said we are going to put into the Azores directly.

The rest of the day was devoted to idleness.

Friday, October 29, 1841

The lookouts reported a ship—the first to be seen since putting to sea. But she was too distant to be hailed. Square-rigged she was, too, they said—just like us.

Saturday, October 30, 1841

We are shipping water somewhere far below on our portside amidship. I do not know exactly where. Mr. Dixwell says it is a minor matter, being a slight leak no doubt caused by that mad whale. There is no need to be alarmed, he told me. I believe him since the pumps have not been set to work. Besides, I have it on the captain's own authority that we shall put into Ponta Delgada in eight days.

A new No. 3 boat was secured to its davits this afternoon. Mr. Benjamin Cook, second boatsteerer and bow oar on Mr. Hansen's boat was given command of the No. 3 boat. However, there was some talk about this and it was decided that Mr. Cook will be boatsteerer of No. 3 and that the captain himself, Mr. Hutchinson, will command her. Mr. James Thomas and Pedro Rua were assigned to the boat as were Mr. John Drummer and Ezra January, landsmen and Henry Clarke, the cooper. By my count that leaves five shipkeepers left to run the *Evening Star* if all three boats are put into the water at the same time.

The new No. 3 crew practice somewhat before sunset.

Sunday, October 31, 1841

A memorial service was held this morning for all those
lost. The captain spoke out each man's name but did not
include Buttons. Instead, he concluded the list by saying
"and all those strangers who since the beginning of time
found their final rest in the ocean deep."

Monday, November 1, 1841

Fifty days—2600 miles from Mystic (so says Gummy).

The air has become noticeably warmer and the sea bluer
during the last several days. Mr. Hutchinson says that
if all goes well we shall reach the port city of Ponta
Delgada on the island of São Miguel in the Azores by
Sunday next.

The captain has become more agreeable. He is more with
the men now than he was before. He smiles much, humors
us all and seems to be happily everywhere at once. I am
more at home, too.

Wednesday, November 3, 1841

The leak has worsened. The pumps have been put to work.
No one seems alarmed. The air is warm; the sea is flat
and blue; we have a good stiff breeze at our backs. Mr.
Dixwell says we shall attend to the damage in port. He
told me that our heading is true; that we are right on
course; and that we are in the southeast drift—a warm
current—northeast of São Miguel and not far off.

Friday, November 5, 1841

We are not running so fast now. We have seen some small
boats and one or two birds. I watched for some sight of

land today but saw none although the air was clear and bright. Mr. Dixwell said that we are making a passage between São Miguel to our northwest and another group of islands to our southeast.

Saturday, November 6, 1841

Land! Land! Land! I awoke this morning to this glorious sight. Land!

We are running very slowly in a westerly course and coming around the southerly reaches of São Miguel. The green and sparkling coast has been on our starboard all day. Oh, what a lovely vision! The Almighty has seen us through. It has been fifty-five days—fifty-five days of fear, cruelty, weather, blistering work and sadness—a restless, hazardous voyage. But tonight I shall sleep well.

Thank you, dear Lord. Thank you for this day.

Sunday, November 7, 1841

We are dead in the water not a few hundred yards offshore.

The captain held the usual Sabbath service early this morning.

There have been a number of small boats circling us from time to time. None have approached too close. Mr. Starkweather says they do not like our smell. I do not think we smell too much.

Later in the morning, a small boat came alongside. Several men came aboard. They were greeted by Mr. Dixwell and Pedro Rua, who speaks the language of these people. They all went below to see the captain. They were not gone long and soon left the ship. Cockeye told me that these men were government officials. They came aboard to inspect the ship's papers, cargo, and whatnot before allowing us to tie up in their port and going ashore. Cockeye also said they probably did none of these things, that he knew the captain well, that he kept the ship's business to himself—something we had all better do—meaning nine men dead, two murdered, that this had better be so if we mean to continue the voyage without official questions and delays.

It is midnight now. I am back in my locker. Mr. Dixwell said I could return here after the No. 3 boat went down with Mr. Goodspeed.

I was on deck for a time watching a few fires on shore. It is warm—no breeze whatever. There is a full moon, much larger than I have ever seen it before. The light from the moon is so bright—even at this late hour—that every small building, every pebble, is plainly visible.

Monday, November 8, 1841

A large boat towed us into the port this morning. We have been tied up since about the noon hour. No one has as yet left the ship except on business—Mr. Hutchinson, Mr. Dixwell, Irish O'Brien, Gummy and Mr. Rua were the only ones.

As soon as we were secure, Mr. Hutchinson sent two divers down—Mr. Thomas and Obadiah Burley—to inspect the hull. It seems that the whale stove in some copper hull sheeting and planking on the portside. The copper loosened enough to allow sea water to come behind it and seep through the cracked planking. Mr. Hansen has taken charge of the repair which is being done from the inside.

Most of the crew spent the better part of the day—me

too—scrubbing down the decks and gear or working on the repair. I was in the forward hold for a while helping Cockeye and Mr. Clarke secure some barrels. We have taken 179 barrels of oil from those two whales.

When Mr. Dixwell returned with the others he allowed me to go into the rigging. I did not go very high and took little notice of the view. I became dizzy and got myself down quickly. Mr. Dixwell and some others were much amused.

Tuesday, November 9, 1841

The first party went ashore today—No. 2 and No. 3 boat crews. Mr. Dixwell said that No. 1 boat and shipkeepers go ashore tomorrow. We should be gone from here by Thursday.

Some of the first party were back before eight bells. The rest came in before sunup. They were all filthy and drunk. Mr. Long, the aft oar on No. 2 was as stiff as a mast. The four who were carrying him toward the ship kept dropping him. He did not stir. They did not pick him up handily being that they themselves were so sotted. Each time they dropped Mr. Long, they got down on their knees and sang a hymn. I counted five hymns.

A most remarkable sight was that of Mr. Curtis, No. 2 boatsteerer.

Mr. Curtis is a giant of a man, standing two heads taller than most. He came down the wharf, drunk like the others, singing very loudly, surrounded by a mob of screaming citizens. It seemed as if a giant was being set upon by a troop of dwarfs. None of this had any affect on him, however. And while the men were pushing, punching and kicking him, a like number of women were

attacking the men. Mr. Curtis finally reached the gangway, shook off his assailants like so many flies, came
aboard and stood at the rail where he blew kisses to the
squirming crowd below. The ladies blew kisses in return,
waved and smiled broadly. The men, for their part, shook
their fists and dragged the ladies out of sight. Mr. Curtis
went below laughing like a madman.

Tomorrow is another day.

Earlier—this afternoon—a British vessel tied up nearby.
She is the *Pegasus* out of Liverpool. She is bound for
Madagascar.

Wednesday, November 10, 1841

It is a wonder that I am still alive. This town is Satan's
residence. It is a noisy, dusty, wicked place—Sodom and
Gomorrah. My late father would sit up in his grave if he
could know what this day was like for me. But I resisted
all temptation.

I left the ship this morning with the No. 1 boat hands
and the shipkeepers. At first we walked up and down the
main street greeting all the ladies. The street is not very
long. In fact the town is not very large. According to Mr.
Dixwell, who has been here before, São Miguel is the
largest of all these Azores islands. It is only some nine
miles wide and about forty miles in length.

Once in a while, we would stop our stroll and look at the
people. At other times some street peddler would stop us
and try to sell us some trinkets or wine or woven baskets
and things like that. Pedro Rua did all of our talking for
us. He understands these people perfectly. However, none
of us bought anything because Mr. Rua would have a
terrible argument with the merchant, followed by a swift

kick a curse or two after which the peddler was sent packing.

This being market day, we finally went to the open-air market at one end of the town. There was a great crowd of people there. It was very lively and colorful. Large crops of bananas, pineapples, fruits of every description were everywhere. There were vegetables, tobacco and flax. And wherever I looked there was a mountain of flowers—brilliant in the sunshine. I bought a couple of bananas and ate them both on the spot. I had a piece of Brutus Hull's pineapple also. It is the first time I had ever tasted any of these fruits. I liked them. All the while we were wandering about the market place most of our party were drinking wine they had bought. They were getting noisier by the minute.

I do not remember how long we remained at the market. Perhaps an hour. I noticed that Mr. Dixwell had gone off somewhere and was no longer in the party. Anyway, we left the market and slowly walked to the other end of town. There was a cool tavern at that end. It was down a narrow alley. It felt good to get out of the sun.

The tavern was already a crowded place. It was filled with local citizens—men and women—more than a dozen Britishers from the *Pegasus,* some Portuguees and more. It was, except for a scuffle or two, a friendly atmosphere.

Before long night came. Few had left the place. More came in. One of the ladies was hoisted onto a table and began to sing a very hollow-sounding sad song. It was more like a wail than a song. Mr. Moses Cummings of our No. 1 boat did not like the sound of it either. He jumped onto another table and began to sing "Yankee Doodle." At that, one of the Britishers jumped onto the table with him and began to sing "God Save the Queen." It was amusing to

92

see this because Mr. Cummings and the Britisher had their arms around each other each trying to sing louder than the other; both trying to sing louder than the lady. Everyone remained in good humor throughout—everyone but the lady.

She became angry. Someone handed her a large pitcher of red wine. With a great heave, she soaked the two singers with it. Everyone cheered. Startled and looking very bloodied, the two sailors lunged across the table—still holding on to each other—and tried to grab the lady who now stood there, in the center of her own table, hands on hips, mocking them with a wild laugh. But the sailors missed their mark and fell down between the tables. There they sat—holding on to each other—dripping wine—stupefied—unable to get their drunken selves to stand.

I do not know if I myself can believe what happened next.

The lady took a long drink of wine, squirting it into her mouth from a bag. When she finished she threw the bag into the crowd. She stood there swaying from side to side and talking to the crowd. Some of the crowd talked back. I did not understand the words. The place became very still. The crowd moved back from the two sotted seamen still sitting on the floor. There was not a sound. The lady moved to the edge of the table. Someone else, nearby, began to sing a slow and sad melody. The lady began to dance. She swayed back and forth, rolling her slim body like an endless ocean wave, never once removing her eyes from the two sailors at her feet. They tried to get up. They reached for the dancing lady only to fall back. As I watched them tumble backward, a large brightly colored cloth sailed through the air and covered both their heads. They quickly pulled it down. It was the dancing lady's dress. She had completely uncovered herself. She was naked.

94

For a moment, all was quiet and still. The only sound was the lonesome voice of the one who was singing. Slowly, the lady started to dance again. But suddenly there was a great explosion of noise. There was shouting and screaming, hand clapping and foot stomping. The crowd started to press against the table. Some of the patrons began to fight. Things began to break. But I tore through that scene and quickly quit the place. I do not know how it shall all end. Even here, in my locker, I can hear the howling of that madhouse.

Thursday, November 11, 1841

We did not depart this day. The repair was not finished to the captain's satisfaction. Now, all is secure.

No one went ashore today for pleasure. Mr. Hutchinson forbade it. He wanted no further trouble of the kind that took place at the tavern last night—events so frightful and wicked that I cannot even write them down. Besides, he wants everything in order. We sail tomorrow.

I overheard the captain tell Mr. Dixwell and Mr. Hansen that there were some stranded New England whalemen on Tenerife in the Canary Islands. They are all that is left of the bark *Good Shepherd,* which caught fire and sank while approaching the islands.

"We could use those men," I heard him say. "We should have a full complement before trying to make a passage around the Horn. It may be our last opportunity for experienced hands."

I learned later that we were heading for the Canaries in any event. The captain was dissatisfied with some of the fruits and vegetables we took on here. He thinks we can do better in the Canaries. He also wants to be certain that the repair will hold.

The Canaries are about one thousand miles to our southeast. The captain plans to make a brief stop before continuing on to the Cape Verde Islands for fresh water. We shall cross the equator from there.

Friday, November 12, 1841

We departed Ponta Delgada on the noon tide today.

Tuesday, November 16, 1841

Nothing to write.

Friday, November 19, 1841

It is warm and breezy topside. It is hot and foul below.

Sunday, November 21, 1841

Seventy days. Mr. Hutchinson held a short service.

Wednesday, November 24, 1841

We are in Santa Cruz de Tenerife. We were secure at sunset. This is a mountainous place. I feel strange.

Thursday, November 25, 1841

Mr. Hansen went ashore today to seek out those whalemen. He reports that no one has seen or heard of such men. We are to depart Saturday with a better food stock. The repair seems adequate.

I do not feel well. I shall feel better once we have some wind behind us and the open sea ahead.

Wednesday, December 22, 1841

I have had a terrible fever they say. I have been on

Tenerife this past month. The *Evening Star* departed these shores without me. Now it is gone—gone from here to the bottom of the sea. I am alone.

I remember being taken off the ship. I remember being brought to this house. These are the events as they happened:

I remember falling to the deck with a burning fever and belly pains the day before the *Evening Star* was to sail. That was on a Friday, November 26. A doctor was called to the ship. He was a passenger on a Spanish vessel tied up nearby. He became alarmed and quickly left the ship. Soon after, some officials came aboard and ordered the captain to quit the port immediately. They were afraid that a terrible plague would be visited upon all of the inhabitants of this island.

Mr. Hutchinson refused to depart. He said that I had not been stricken with a plague; that he had not finished his business. The officials then had the lines cut and a towboat pulled us away from the port. I was still aboard and feeling a little better.

But Mr. Hutchinson was no longer certain that I was not stricken with a plague. He did not want to chance infesting his ship. He had had enough trouble on the voyage as it was.

Late that night—we were still in the port waters having dropped anchor after the towboat returned to the wharf—the captain sent Ezra January to my locker with orders for me to collect my gear and be prepared to leave the ship. I did this after which I returned to my blanket shaking with fits of chill. It was hot in my locker—I knew that—but I was fearfully cold.

Some minutes later Ezra entered the locker and picked

100

up me and my sea bag, being careful to see that I was still wrapped in the blanket. He carried me to the starboard gangway. I was too weak to protest. I would have liked to continue the voyage. There I heard Mr. Hutchinson order Mr. Dixwell to make certain arrangements with the elderly couple I now find myself with—Señor and Señora Juán Deseda. They were to see to it that I regained my health—if at all—without arousing the local people with my presence. These people were to see to it that I secured a work passage on another American vessel whenever convenient.

Ezra put me in a boat. Everyone was there. They were all kind and wished me well. Someone placed a scrimshaw whale tooth in the blanket. It had two whales carved into it. The boat was swung out and lowered away. I was secretly rowed to a desolate beach. All the while we quietly slipped toward shore, Mr. Dixwell said many things to me. I remember none of it now. I recall saying some things to him. I cannot remember these either.

We remained on that beach for some time—for how long I do not known. Mr. Dixwell went off to make the arrangements. I was unconscious and near death when he returned.

I remained in that state for several days and when I awakened I was here—in this hut—and the men were gone. For several weeks after, my situation was desperate. I was even too ill and weak to pray.

Señora Deseda never left my side. It was not until two or three days ago that I have felt well enough to rise from my bed. I am much better today and well enough to write all this down.

I have been thinking all day about the *Evening Star* with good cause. Last night, Señor Deseda returned from the

village with the awful news that the *Evening Star* was lost at sea with all hands. He learned this from a sailor who arrived only yesterday morning. This sailor told Señor Deseda that there was a great storm off South America's eastern coast about 10 degrees south of the equator. His vessel was caught in the storm. She was northward bound when the storm broke upon them. The storm changed their course for them as they were helplessly driven westward toward the coastal city of Recife in Brazil.

At the height of the storm, swore the sailor, they spotted the *Evening Star* a few points off their port beam. At first she was very close and unable to control her own motion. But the blasting wind and mountainous waves drove them farther apart. Neither ship was able to hail the other due to the roar of the storm. However, the two ships were so close in one perilous moment that the name EVENING STAR MYSTIC CONNECTICUT was plainly seen across her transom. Not long after, as the two ships were moving farther apart, a great wave struck the *Evening Star*. She listed so far over on her portside that she was unable to right herself. A few minutes later she rolled completely over and sank out of sight. It was the end of her. Oh my God, why was I spared?

Señor Deseda finished the account by saying that the storm ended shortly after the *Evening Star* went down. The sea became calm. The other vessel, damaged as she was, remained afloat—right side up. She cruised about for a while looking for survivors. There were none.

Friday, December 24, 1841

Tomorrow is Christmas. Were it only a New England Christmas. Señor and Señora Deseda have been very kind

to me. They are old and gentle people. Señora Deseda speaks no English. But Señor Deseda speaks my language plainly.

In all this time that they have cared for me, there has been little conversation between us, however.

I trust that I shall leave this place soon.

My thoughts have been on the *Evening Star*. Everyone of the crew is alive in my head. I cannot rid myself of their faces.

Saturday, December 25, 1841

Christmas. Why do I suffer so? I am alive and well. What joy is there for me on this day? What joy is there for my dear mother, for my sisters on this day? Is there any joy for the *Evening Star* in the hereafter?

Tuesday, December 28, 1841

Señor Deseda has made an arrangement. I am to go to sea again. We went down to the wharf today and spoke with the ship's master, Captain Jason Hull. He is an uncle of Brutus Hull, late of the *Evening Star*. I told him all that I knew about the end of that ship. He had heard about it too. He is a kindly man.

His ship—now my ship—is a whaler, the *Martha B. Dodson,* out of New Bedford. She is southward bound. Captain Hull said he was shorthanded but not for a ship's boy. He already has one, Billy Little. He asked me if I was ready to do a man's work and if so he would sign me on as an ordinary seaman. My lay would be $1/175$. I told him I was ready. I agreed to the terms. He told me to be ready to come aboard tomorrow morning as soon after sunrise as possible. The ship will sail Friday next.

I thanked him properly and returned with Señor Deseda to the hut.

I do not know how or with what I can show my gratitude to Señor and Señora Deseda. As near as I can figure they have no other family on this island. They spoke of some children but I have never seen them. I think they have looked upon me as their son.

Tomorrow I shall leave them. I shall give them my scrimshaw bone.

Now I begin again.

EPILOGUE

I thanked him properly and returned with Senor Deseda to the hut.

I do not know how or with what I can show my gratitude to Senor and Senora Deseda. As near as I can figure they have no family on this island. They spoke of some children but I have never seen them. I think they have looked upon me as their son.

Tomorrow I shall leave them. I shall give them my scrimshaw bone.

Now I begin again!

There was no further writing—no further word—from Jeremiah Poole. Certainly none was included in the storm-soaked package handed to me by that terrifying figure who called himself "Charlie Poole," onetime keeper of the Norton's Point Lighthouse in Sea Gate.

However, I was not altogether satisfied that this would be all I should ever know. More recently, I decided to make as thorough a search as possible in the hope that I could find some clue—some scrap—anything—that would shed additional light on the saga of Jeremiah Poole.

To begin with, the person of Jeremiah Poole is an established fact. There is a copy of a death certificate and a last will and testament that had been filed for probate in the courts of New Bedford, Massachusetts, shortly after Jeremiah Poole was laid to rest in the sea east of Sandy Hook, New Jersey. These and other papers reveal that Captain Jeremiah Poole was not only master of the whaleship *Pandora* at the time of his death, he was also the ship's owner. Strangely, the will makes no mention whatever of any direct heir—no wife, no children! All of Jeremiah Poole's property, which consisted of the ship, various papers, cash, a bank account and some small keepsakes, was bequeathed to his two surviving sisters—Sarah Poole Trumbull, a widow, and Rachel Poole, a spinster. They promptly sold the vessel. She was never heard from again. Sarah passed on during the following year, 1902. Rachel died in 1910.

My thoughts soon turned to Jeremiah's first ship, *Evening Star*. Thus far, I have been unable to find any record of her—nothing to indicate where she was built, by whom she was built, or whether she ever existed at all. Moreover, I have been unable to discover any information about Charles Lockwood, the ship's owner, or any of the officers and men in his employ who sailed aboard the *Evening Star*. It is as

113

if they too never existed.

None of this is unusual. Few records were kept in those days. Those records that were kept could have been lost.

Yet, I was not prepared for the mystifying information I managed to uncover next—and this I learned only within the past day or two:

The United States Lighthouse Service has no record of anyone by the name of Poole in its file. Neither does the United States Coast Guard or the United States Department of the Treasury, under whose authorities the Lighthouse Service operates.

Astonishing, too, is the news that there is no naval service record for anyone by the name of Amos Poole—Admiral Amos Poole!

This cannot be! It is impossible! There must be an error somewhere which I am certain will be discovered soon. After all, I saw these men. I knew one of them—Amos—quite well. I had long talks with him. Why, there was that 1946 New York *Times* notice of the death of ninty-one-year-old Amos Poole, Admiral USN, retired. Needless to say, I did not let that particular recollection go by without checking it. I have just spent hours pouring over every single issue of the *Times* for the year 1946 on file at the New York Public Library. There was no such notice! Perhaps I never saw it at all.

I have no explanation for any of this—none that would be logical, at any rate. Surely, Jeremiah's will does not indicate that a son, Amos, ever existed. But he may have had his own reasons for ignoring the fact. If Jeremiah did indeed have a son and, later, a grandson—that would have been Charlie—it is quite possible that a series of unfortunate coincidences has arisen, leaving no record of their lives. I have no idea what these coincidences might be.

However, there is one footnote to this story that keeps me from losing my sanity altogether.

During my travels to discover what I could about Jeremiah Poole and the *Evening Star,* I managed to collect numerous papers, pamphlets, books—anything that would have some bearing on the project—even a whale's tooth—for whatever purpose it would have. Some of these papers—those that had no particular value—are in their original form. Others—those of value and being the property of others—I had photographically copied.

Among these papers, surprising as it may seem, is a photostat copy of the "settlement of voyage" of the *Martha B. Dodson.* The settlement was dated December 9, 1844.

I had been everywhere between Sea Gate, Brooklyn, New York, and Nantucket Island off the Massachusetts coast— New Haven, Mystic, New London, Niantic, Pawcatuck, and other places in Connecticut; Newport and Providence in Rhode Island; New Bedford, Boston, Salem in Massachusetts and several places on Martha's Vineyard, another island off the Massachusetts coast. Yet, I cannot remember where I found this revealing document.

In any event, the settlement of voyage of the *Martha B. Dodson,* Jason Hull, ship's master, indicates that all hands returned to New Bedford. She had been at sea three years, two months, eleven days. The *Martha B.* brought home a cargo of 1589 barrels of sperm oil, 431 barrels of right whale oil and 4500 pounds of whale bone.

Included in the list of officers and crew was the name "Jeremy Poole, ordinary seaman." Jeremiah "Jeremy" Poole—now seventeen years old—received as his lay $676 less $10.12 in "miscellany" charges he had incurred during the voyage. His share—as he had written it would be—was $\frac{1}{175}$ of the profits.

Settlement of Voyage. Ship Martha B. Dodson
New Bedford December 9, 1844

Name	Rate	Lay	Share	Ship's Bill
Jason Hull	Master	1/15	$7,886.67	
John Arnold	Mate	1/18	6,572.23	
Samuel Chase	2nd Mate	1/50	2,366.67	
Wm. Foote	3rd Mate	1/60	1,971.67	$18.22
Chs. Jones	Boatsteerer	1/75	1,577.33	
Robert Coley	Boatsteerer	1/80	1,478.75	24.00
Jonah Nash	Boatsteerer	1/85	1,391.78	
Geoffrey Kert	Cooper	1/75	1,577.33	
Wm. Ball	2nd Cooper	1/150	787.67	
James Short	Blacksmith	1/75	1,577.33	
Jeremy Poole	Ord. Seaman	1/175	676.00	10.12
Amos Woody	Seaman	1/160	739.31	
Ths. Bill	Seaman	1/160	739.31	
Abraham Reed	Seaman	1/160	739.31	18.00
Edw. Peabody	Seaman	1/160	739.31	
George Potts	Seaman	1/160	739.31	
Richard James	Seaman	1/160	739.31	
Ambrose Gregg	Seaman	1/160	739.31	

Jeremiah Poole returned home a good deal richer than he had counted on. Not only that, he was alive—a lucky lone survivor of a lost whaleship.

Obviously, Jeremiah Poole returned to the sea and remained there for the rest of his life. Yet, I cannot help but believe that his first lonesome encounter with the sea was so shocking an experience for a boy of his sensitive qualities and education that he was never able to live out his long life happily ever after. Not even in his own death—sixty years later, joined at last to his first sailing companions in that same watery grave—did his torment seem to cease.

One may speculate all he likes about every aspect of these episodes—Jeremiah's voyage aboard two different whaling vessels, my own mystifying experiences surrounding all of this—but one thing is most apparent to me. Jeremiah Poole, for reasons best known to himself, never told a living soul about life—his or anyone else's—aboard the *Evening Star*. He never reported the crimes, plots and injustices that unfolded above and below and beyond her greasy decks during the short ill-fated voyage. He simply put all of the sordid details out of his mind and buried everyone—the good and the bad—in the briny deep off Recife, Brazil. "Let it be the end of it," I can almost hear him mutter to himself. And, as he himself had written at the very end, "Now I begin again."

Surely, not one word about the disastrous loss of the *Evening Star* appeared in any of the few newspapers of the time. There was no maritime court of inquiry convened to certify the loss, determine the cause, fix responsibility or investigate the deaths of nine men that occurred at sea, if, by some chance word of these events filtered back to New England after the *Evening Star* made her stops at Ponta Delgada and Tenerife.

The fact that the *Evening Star* went down in a violent storm off South America while on an outbound southwesterly course seems to have been no secret.

Curiously, too, the *Evening Star* never hailed or was herself hailed by any vessel while at sea. Except for the small boats around the islands, the several that were in port, the one distant ship that Jeremiah mentions in his journal along with the vessel that the *Evening Star* closed in on during the storm, she seems to have traveled a lonely course.

In any event, all during his lifetime, Jeremiah must have wondered how he could permit the last months of the lives of thirty-three men to disappear with hardly a trace—without so much as a whispered accounting of their deeds and misdeeds. There were innocent men aboard that ship—Buttons, for one—Buttons, the shanghaiied, murdered peddler from Mystic and other places. In the interest of justice, God-fearing Jeremiah Poole was the only one to survive who could tell the story and he did not. Perhaps he made a promise to Mr. Dixwell while he was being put ashore at Tenerife—a promise made during a hushed conversation between the two that Jeremiah claimed not to remember—a promise to keep his silence until the *Evening Star* returned. This we shall never know.

Whatever the truth of the matter, it is difficult for me to resist the idea that long-gone Jeremiah Poole decided to tell the story. And from somewhere far away, and in a manner both mysterious and supernatural—believe what you will—Jeremiah Poole made me the instrument of his conscience.

Now the story is told. I have done his bidding. I trust this will be the end of it. Somehow, I doubt it.

AUTHOR BIOGRAPHY

Leonard Everett Fisher, painter, illustrator, author and educator, was born and raised in New York City. His formal art training began at the Heckscher Foundation in 1932 and was completed after his wartime military service at the Yale Art School, from which he received a Master of Fine Arts degree and the Winchester Fellowship. He had studied previously with Moses Soyer, Reginald Marsh, Olindo Ricci, and Serge Chermayeff. In 1950, Mr. Fisher received a Pulitzer Art Fellowship. He spent much of that year in Europe, returning home in 1951 to become dean of the Whitney School of Art in New Haven, Connecticut. He resigned from that post in 1953 and turned his attention to children's literature. Since then he has illustrated approximately two hundred children's books, about twenty of which he has written. He has received numerous citations, and in 1968 he was awarded the Premio Grafico for juvenile illustration by the International Book Fair, Bologna, Italy—the only American thus honored. Books containing his illustrations have been published in a variety of foreign languages and distributed throughout the world by the United States Information Agency. Mr. and Mrs. Fisher and their three children live in Westport, Connecticut.